I DON'T LIKE POETRY

First published 2016 by
Bloomsbury Education, an imprint of Bloomsbury Publishing Plc
50 Bedford Square, London, WC1B 3DP

www.bloomsbury.com

Bloomsbury is a registered trademark of Bloomsbury Publishing Plc

A CIP catalogue for this book is available from the British Library

ISBN 978-1-4729-3003-3

Typeset by Becky Chilcott
Printed and bound by CPI Group (UK) Ltd, Croydon CR0 4YY

1 3 5 7 9 10 8 6 4 2

MIX
Paper from
responsible sources
FSC
www.fsc.org   FSC® C020471

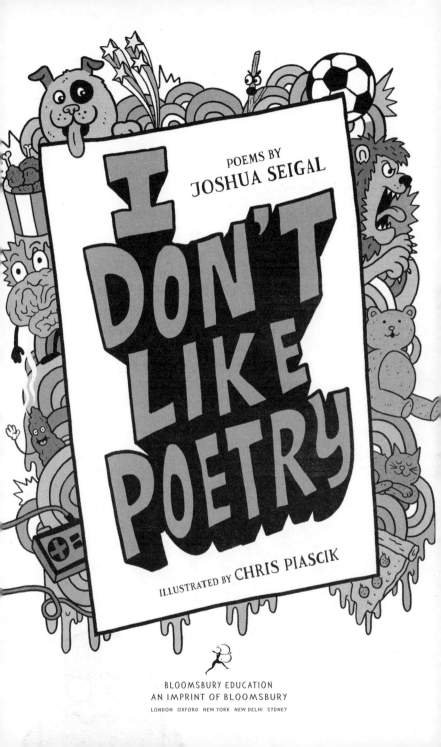

POEMS BY
JOSHUA SEIGAL

I DON'T LIKE POETRY

ILLUSTRATED BY CHRIS PIASCIK

BLOOMSBURY EDUCATION
AN IMPRINT OF BLOOMSBURY
LONDON OXFORD NEW YORK NEW DELHI SYDNEY

Contents

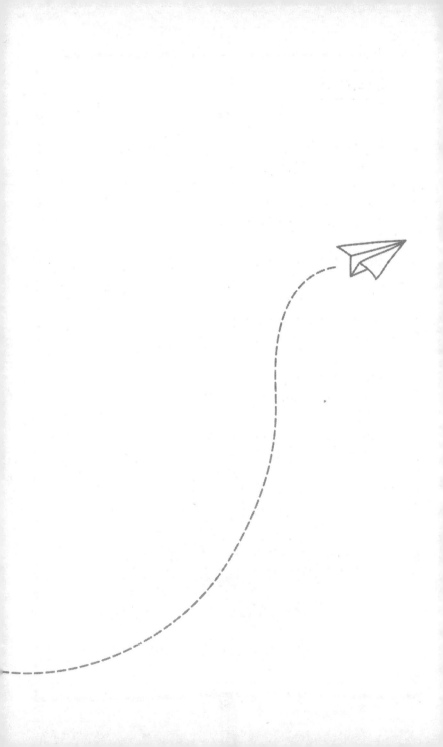

Untitled

The title of this poem,
it will really catch your eye.

The title of this poem
doesn't even need to try.

The title of this poem
is the best one in the book.

The title of this poem
is amazing – come and look!

The title of this poem
will astound you, that's for sure;

you'll convulse in sheer wonder
and start rolling on the floor.

The title of this poem
is the finest. None is greater.

The title of this poem is…
I'll think of something later.

Resolutions

DAY 1

I won't be late for school again.
I won't swing in my seat.
I'll do my best on every test
and I will never cheat.

I'll help with chores around the house.
I won't get in a rage.
I'll get a broom and sweep my room
and clean the hamster's cage.

I'll put my money in the bank.
I won't spend it on sweets.
I'll make a pledge to eat more veg
and give up eating meat.

I'll go out jogging round the park.
I'll try hard to get fit.
I will not shirk, I'll do the work
and I will never quit.

I'll be the best that I can be,
improve in every way.
I will shine bright, and I will write
a poem every day!

DAY 2

I Don't Like Poetry

I don't like similes.
Every time I try to think of one
my brain feels like a vast, empty desert;
my eyes feel like raisins floating in an ocean;
my fingers feel like sweaty sausages.

I don't like metaphors.
Whenever I attempt them
a hammer starts beating in my chest;
lava starts bubbling in my veins;
zombies have a fight in my stomach.

I don't like alliteration.
We learnt about it in school
but it's seriously, stupendously silly;
definitely drastically difficult;
terribly, troublingly tricky.

I don't like onomatopoeia.
I wish I could blow it up
with a ZAP! and a BANG! and a CRASH!;
a BOOM! and a CLANG! and a POW!;
a CLASH! and a BAM! and a THUD!

And I don't like repetition
I don't like repetition
I don't like repetition...

4

Multiple Choice

1. Always do your very best
   with the answers on the

   (A) Test
   (B) Toilet
   (C) Inside of your nostrils

2. I've told you twenty-thousand times –
   write the answers out in

   (A) Rhymes
   (B) Japanese
   (C) Mashed potato

3. I've said it before and I'll say it again –
   write the answers with a

   (A) Pen
   (B) Frown
   (C) Dead centipede

4. Let this be your final warning –
   concentrate and stop that

   (A) Yawning
   (B) Pigeon
   (C) Runaway train

5. I've been driven round the bend!
Now the test is at an

(A) End
(B) Egg
(C) Elephant's underpants

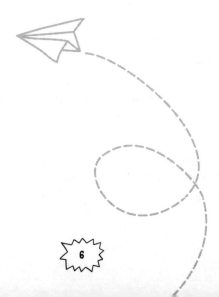

Fun Poem

This is a fun poem.
I demand that you enjoy it.
If you are not having fun then you
have to stay behind and write lines:
I must have more fun.
I must have more fun.
I must have more fun.

This is a fun poem.
If you find your mind wandering off
then you deserve a swift smack
on the back of the head –
not everyone has the privilege
of reading poems as fun as this.
Some people are forced
to read *boring* poems, written by men
who died centuries ago. Not you!
You are the lucky ones,
so sit still, be quiet
and appreciate it.

Now feel the fun wafting through your nostrils –
in, out, in, out, in, out, in, out –

and in and out of your lungs –
in, out, in, out, in, out, in, out...

You will be tested tomorrow on how much fun you've had.
That'll be fun, won't it?
WHAT DO YOU MEAN YOU'RE NOT HAVING FUN?!

Well, in that case, you need to try harder –
we get out what we put in.

F.U.N.P.O.E.M.

Repeat after me:
F.U.N.P.O.E.M!

Now repeat it until home time:
F.U.N.P.O.E.M! F.U.N.P.O.E.M!
F.U.N.P.O.E.M! F.U.N.P.O.E.M...

Just a Book?

It's a letter in a bottle
bobbing blindly in the sea,
it's a verdant leaf in summer
hanging halfway up a tree,
it's a pebble sleeping softly
in a gently flowing brook
but it's never, no it's never,
no it's *never* just a book.

It's the topping on your pizza
as it sits upon your plate,
it's the fish that you've been after
as you hook it with your bait,
it's a cupboard of ingredients
all waiting for the cook
but it's never, no it's never,
no it's *never* just a book.

It's a soldier in a battle
as he launches a grenade,
it's a hunter in a forest
as she sharpens up her blade,
it's a playmate, it's a bully,
it's a policeman, it's a crook
but it's never, no it's never,
no it's *never* just a book.

It's a parcel of ideas,
it's a package full of tools,
it's a field full of freedom,
it's a folder full of rules,
it's a fancy flight of fantasy
so come and have a look –
see it's never, no it's never,
no it's *never* just a book!

Boys Can

Who can take words and
make them prowl and play,
make them growl and shout,
make them spit wild rhymes
and make them run about?
Boys can.

Who can build castles
and fill oceans with words,
use sentences as swords,
use metaphors as bricks
and make paragraphs do tricks?
Boys can.

Who can kick words around
like footballs,
cuddle up to books like kittens,
race letters round a track
and eat stories like a snack?
Boys can.

Boys – with words you can build
houses bigger and more important
than anything your hands
could handle.
Fill your toolboxes with them.
You have the power.

Summing Girls Up

girl + determination = mathematician
girl − preconception = builder
girl x stamina = athlete
girl + girl = friend

girl x motivation = scientist
girl − stereotype = plumber
(girl + girl) ÷ jealousy = loneliness
girl + freedom = anything

(By Joshua Seigal and Carrie Esmond)

Funny Haiku

ha ha ha ha ha
ha ha ha ha ha ha ha
ha ha ha ha ha

Dog Haiku

Woof woof growl yap growl
Growl snarl woof woof yap woof snarl
Howl growl snarl woof woof

How to Make a Dog

Your mum won't let you get a dog?
Well, here is what you do:
You make a dog all by yourself!
Sounds crazy, but it's true.

Just get yourself some paper
and procure yourself a pen,
then sit down in a quiet spot
and draw a head, and then

a fluffy body, legs and tail.
Yes, draw the whole caboodle.
Congratulations on your dog!
You have a labradoodle.

Dog on the Ceiling

Some say that he's a demon,
some say that he's a freak,
but if you saw my little dog
you'd know that he's unique.

He sleeps upon the ceiling,
just like a bat you see.
He hangs up there all day and night
defying gravity.

Some say that it's a miracle,
some say it can't be done,
but my dog snoozes up above –
I guess he thinks it's fun.

This evidence will show you
he's the strangest dog in town!

What's that? You mean you're telling me
the picture's upside down?

Tell it to the Dog

If you have had
an awful day
and no one wants
to come and play
and all your woes
won't go away,
just tell it to the dog.

If everybody
picks on you
and all your plans
have fallen through;
if you feel lonely,
sad and blue,
just tell it to the dog.

Dogs do not judge.
They understand.
They rub your leg.
They lick your hand.
If you feel lost
in no-man's land
just tell it to the dog.

Dogs keep your secrets
safe within.
They don't care if
you lose or win.
So turn that frown
into a grin
and tell it to the dog!

(Or, failing that,
make do with the cat...)

Animal House

There's an **ARMY** of **HERRINGS** in my bath,
and a **BEVY** of **OTTERS** too.
There's a **BOOGLE** of **WEASELS**
under my easel,
and an **IMPLAUSIBILITY** of **GNUS**.

There's a **LAMENTATION** of **SWANS**,
and a **MURMURATION** of **STARLINGS**,
and a **MURDER** of **CROWS**
in my sink.
There's a **FLAMBOYANCE** of **FLAMINGOS**
in my underwear drawer,
which is rather odd, I think!

There's a **PARCEL** of **PENGUINS** in my fridge,
and a **SHIVER** of **SHARKS** in my bowl.
There's a **MOB** of **MEERKATS** under the rug,
along with a **LABOUR** of **MOLES**.

There's a **PARLIAMENT** of **OWLS**,
and a **PANDEMONIUM** of **PARROTS**,
and a **KNOB** of **TOADS**
on my pillow,
and in my boxes
there's a **SKULK** of **FOXES**
and a **HOOVER** of **ARMADILLOS**.

Lying in my bed,
so still they're almost dead,
there's a **LAZINESS** of **SLOTHS**,
and if you open up my shed
they'll be flying round your head –
a **UNIVERSE** of **MOTHS**!

I've a **BIKE** of **WASPS** in my trousers,
nibbling at my bottom,
while a **COALITION** of **CHEETAHS**
chase a **DAZZLE** of **ZEBRAS**
down the hall – I think they got 'em!
And into my toilet I dare not go –
there's an **OBSTINACY** of **BUFFALO**.

A **COMMITTEE** of **VULTURES** circles the ceiling
and if you want to know how I'm really feeling,
well, I like my varied company,
but the thing I most like to do,
is to go down the road
and to look at the **CROWD** of **HUMANS**
in the zoo!

Warrior King

I'm the Warrior King of the garden.
I'm a revolutionary,
with my gun and my axe and my telescope
and my lookout in the tree.

I'm the Warrior King of the garden.
I'm a soldier, a fighter, a winner.
I don't take orders from anyone
until Mum calls me in for dinner.

Gamer

I'm a zombie–zapping fighter,
I'm a prowling–through–the–nighter,
you will find no mind that's brighter –
I send demons to their doom.

I'm a sportsman, I'm a racer,
I'm a rider, I'm a chaser,
I swing swords and I shoot lasers
and I never leave my room.

I have faced a thousand armies,
rolling boulders do not harm me,
I drive other players barmy
wishing they could be the same.

When I'm overthrowing nations
there will be no hesitation,
this is total domination –
don't tell me it's just a game.

But my clothes are getting smelly
and I'm growing quite a belly
and I'm staring at the telly
as my mind begins to crack,

and my eyes are getting squarer
and my friends are getting rarer
and my world is getting barer.
Where's my life? I want it back.

The dance of the heart

                    The gulp of the throat

      The threep of the whistle

The roar of the crowd

      The crunch of the tackle

        The bark from the sidelines

      The skim on the pass

        The crack of the shot

            The swoosh of the net

        The whoop of your dad

The squeeze of the hug

        The music of joy

22

My Favourite Thing

You
are my favourite thing
in the whole world.
Well, you
and my sheep
and my tree.
And I quite like
the twenty–first letter
of the alphabet.
So I guess you could say
my favourite things
are you, ewe, yew and U.

Short Sharp Poem

I went into the short sharp shop
I went there after dark
And I received a short sharp shock
From the short shop shark.

Otter Letters

I gotta getta lotta letters
for a lotta little otters –
whatta lotta little letters
I had better get.
The problem with a lotta letters
for a lotta little otters
is the lotta litter little letters
leave when wet.

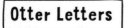

Love Letter to a Lychee

Oh lychee, I love you so!
Your spiky skin hides the wonderful, sweet flesh within,
like a mysterious cloak covering many secrets.
When I put you in my mouth I taste laughter and joy.
Oh lychee, you smell like a little piece of heaven!
I want to roll in a bath with you and to sleep in a bed
made out of your devilish delightful deliciousness.
When I'm with you I feel like the world is a place
of rainbows and honey;
all other fruit is nothing compared to you.
I love every inch of you,

but your heart is made of stone.

M

Addicted To Chicken

Bwark! Bwark!
I'm addicted to chicken!
Bwark! Bwark!
I'm addicted to chicken!
Bwark! Bwark!
I'm addicted to chicken!

My brow starts sweating and pulse starts to quicken

Nobody knows the pleasure I feel
At the thought of a greasy fried chicken meal
I pass the chicken shop and my heart skips a beat
I'll eat the freaky creature from the beak to the feet
I'll slurp the luscious legs and the wicked, wicked wing
For chicken is my life, it's my everything, 'cos

Bwark! Bwark!
I'm addicted to chicken!
Bwark! Bwark!
I'm addicted to chicken!
Bwark! Bwark!
I'm addicted to chicken!

My teeth are chewin' and my tongue is lickin'

I'll have it with some coke and I'll have it with some chips
I'll have it with some sauce that oozes and drips
I'll have it with some friends, they're as crazy as me

26

And we'll have ourselves a little fried chicken spree
So listen to me now as I spread my wicked word
There's nothing I won't do for a bit of battered bird, 'cos

Bwark! Bwark!
I'm addicted to chicken!
Bwark! Bwark!
I'm addicted to chicken!
Bwark! Bwark!
I'm addicted to chicken!

My chin starts to double and my waist starts to thicken

When I see a chicken burger I really wanna hug it
My brain is turning into a giant chicken nugget
I'm gonna move my bed down to the chicken shop
So even when I go to sleep I won't have to stop
I'm gonna swap my clothes for a piece of chicken skin
Get a funnel for my mouth to drop the chicken in
In fact I'll hook a drip right up to my veins
For the chicken lickin' life's got me goin' insane, 'cos

Bwark! Bwark!
I'm addicted to chicken!
Bwark! Bwark!
I'm addicted to chicken!
Bwark! Bwark!
I'm addicted to chicken!

Bwark! Bwark!
I'm addicted to CHICKEN!

Edible Bedroom

My bed is made of apple pie,
the finest known to man.
My lights are made of blueberries,
my books from marzipan.

My desk is made of marble cake.
My sink is made of jelly.
A great big blob of mayonnaise
is plonked inside my telly.

My carpet's made of pizza
and my curtains from salami.
My pillow's stuffed with apricots,
enough to feed an army.

My mattress is a slab of cheese.
My shelves are made of meat.
You may think with a room like this
my life is far from sweet.

With covers made of candyfloss
all tangled in a heap,
You may think I'd go bonkers
from a total lack of sleep.

It's true my room is crazy.
It's not easy to relax,
but when I find it hard to snooze
I've lots of midnight snacks.

Eating the Stars

The night is a trawler,
sprawling its catch
across the sky.

I'm in the back garden,
eating the stars.

I reach across to pluck
a warm, white orb,
sensing its smoothness
on the back of my tongue;
the chilli-pepper pang
as it fizzes in my stomach.

I twist a comet's tail
round my fork like spaghetti,
scoop out a supernova
with my spoon,
use my knife
to slice open the moon.

Inside, Mum and Dad
hurl angry words like meteors.

I sit alone at my table,
feasting on the universe.

The Hungry One

1 8 2
1 8 3
1 8 4
1 8 5
1 8 6
1 8 7
1 8 8 &
1 8 9!

A One-Word Poem That, For Some Strange Reason Which the Finest Minds Known to Humanity Are Yet to Comprehend, Can Make a Room Full of Small Children Laugh

Poo

A Two-Word Poem (At a Stretch)

Fantastic

E   l   a   s   t   i   c

A Cross Stick

Sometimes people chuck me about

Today a dog chewed me

It makes me really angry

Can't everybody just leave me alone?

Killers of nature, they are!

Lovely Little Poem

I'm a lovely little poem.
I'm as timid as a mouse.
I'm squeaking and I'm creaking
through the pages of my house.

I'm a lovely little poem.
I'm snoozing in your book.
I'm like a dainty dragonfly –
come and have a look.

I'm a lovely little poem.
I help you when you're sad.
I'm a cute and cuddly kitten.
I'm the friend you never had.

I'm a lovely little poem.
I'm a whisper in your dream.
Come on in and wake me up...

listen to me

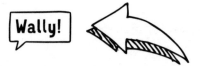

Wally!

I forgot to tape my favourite show
Didn't finish the milk in my cereal bowl
Only wore a thin t-shirt when it was cold
What am I?
YOU'RE A WALLY!

I got ink stains on my brand new fleece
Walked down the road and got chased by geese
Had some chocolate and dropped the very last piece
What am I?
YOU'RE A WALLY!

I put my pants on the wrong way round
Tried to burp really quietly but did it too loud
Came last in the test and feeling quite proud
What am I?
YOU'RE A WALLY!

I went swimming in my sister's bikini
Dropped crumbs in my uncle's Lambourghini
Overturned my mum's martini
What am I?
YOU'RE A WALLY!

I swapped my dog for a packet of crisps
Retook a penalty and I still missed
Drive my teachers round the twist
What am I?
YOU'RE A WALLY!

So I wrote this poem to keep me in line
Got to the end, tried to think of a rhyme
But couldn't think of what to say
What am I?
... YOU'RE A WALLY!

Zombie Poem

What's slushy and what's mushy
and so very good to eat?
What's wobbly and knobbly
and is a tasty treat?
What is it that I dream of
when I'm shambling down the street?
It's brains brains brains brains
BRRRRRAINS!

What is that goo that's greyish-blue,
that thing I love to munch?
What is it that I slurp on
when I sit down to my lunch?
What has a soggy texture
blended with a pleasant crunch?
It's brains brains brains brains
BRRRRRAINS!

What is that thing that gives you life
and lives inside your head?
What is it that I'll nick from you
as you lie in your bed?
What are those tasty morsels
that I need to keep me fed?
They're brains brains brains brains
BRRRRRAINS!

What is it that your teacher has
that makes her very smart?
What makes her good at languages
and history and art?
What is it that'll I'll gobble up
before the lesson starts?
Her brains brains brains brains
BRRRRRAINS!

But chewing them is tiring
and I need some time to play.
I need some relaxation,
yes I need to get away.
Where is it that I'll travel to
for my holiday?

It's Spain Spain Spain Spain
SPPPAAAIINNN!!!

Dracula's Love Letter

I'll feast on your tongue in a sandwich.
I'll gobble your teeth in a pie.
I'll boil your lips
and I'll scoff them with chips
then I'll munch on the back of your thigh.

I'll gnaw on your neck for my breakfast.
I'll chew on your chin for my tea.
I'll grind down your bones
to make sweet eyes–cream cones
then I'll gulp down a spleen kedgeree.

I'll build a baguette with your bottom.
I'll cook up a stew with your toes.
I'll crush up your shoulder blade,
drink it with mucusade,
then I'll devour your nose.

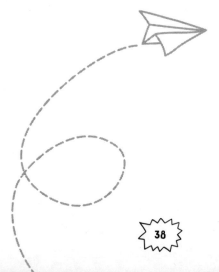

I'll pick off the flesh from your ribcage.
I'll slurp on the wax from your ear.
I'll chomp on your flab
as I make a kebab
using all that remains of your rear.

I'll guzzle your guts for my supper,
and then on your blood I will sup.
There ain't no one who is
as pretty as you is –
I just want to eat you all up.

Goo

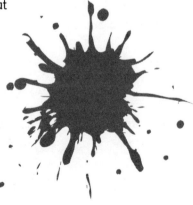

I don't mind gunk
I don't mind slush
I don't mind gunge
I don't mind mush

I don't mind filth
I don't mind slime
I don't mind sludge
I don't mind grime

I don't mind gloop
I don't mind muck
I don't mind ooze
I don't mind yuck –

These things are fine,
But this is true:
You just can't beat
A bit of GOO!

My Neighbour Owns a Lion

My neighbour owns a lion.
It lives out in his shed.
I sometimes hear it roaring
when I'm lying in my bed.

It roams among the flowers.
It paces up and down.
My neighbour's lion surely is
the only one in town.

Sometimes he plays fetch with it,
but not with sticks, with logs.
He doesn't feed it from a tin,
he feeds it cats and dogs.

The lion's always hungry.
It prowls in search of prey.
In fact my neighbour's lion
caught a burglar yesterday.

My neighbour owns a lion.
It's ready to attack,
but my ball is in his garden...
will you help me get it back?

Team Earth

My uncle Graham
believes in aliens.
I used to think he was stupid
but I don't anymore –

think of sport:
every few years,
during the World Cup,
we forget the teams
we usually support
and start cheering whole countries,
with their players
brought together
from lots of different teams.

But wouldn't it be better
if the world *itself*
could form a team,
made up of players
from different countries,
cultures, colours and creeds?

You might say there'd be no one
for this team to play against.
But what if there were aliens?

If there were aliens
the world would have to unite,
arm in arm for the Great
Intergalactic
Penalty Shootout.

So now I think
I like the thought
that uncle Graham's right.
I like the thought
that the stars
we see at night
harbour aliens,
bringing us together.

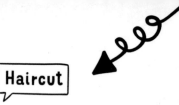

Haircut

When Mum gets scissors from their case
My heart goes wild and starts to race

I sit down on a kitchen chair
She starts to tinker with my hair

Hacking at my silky mane
She thinks it is some kind of game –

She's never had one day of training
But her vigour can't be reined in.

Giggling as she nicks my ear
She says I have nothing to fear

She snips away so recklessly
I fear for my sanity

She seems to think it is a hoot!
Then she'll reveal her labour's fruit:

A haircut that she thinks is funky.
But I look more like a monkey.

Leaning on the windowsill
She smiles at her self-taught skill;

Her new book *really* worries me –
Beginner's Guide to Dentistry...

My Grandpa's Beard

It's like a dead otter attached to his chin.
It looks like a furry grey stoat.
It billows and tumbles its way round his face
going up to his ears
and down past his throat.

I wonder: at night, does it judder to life
as he lies all tucked up in his bed?
Does it tap out a tango and do a backflip?
Does it fight with the hairs
on the top of his head?

Does it sneak from his face and jump down to the floor
and curl under the bed like a cat?
Does it sprout a malevolent pair of wings?
Does it swoop round the room
like a woolly grey bat?

I shudder to think of the hairs in his sink –
I doubt he'd have need of a plug.
He should gather it up and then he could cash in
and sell all the hairs
to turn into a rug.

For my grandpa's beard's a sight to behold
as it dangles half way down his sweater.
Some say it's the greatest that ever was grown...

but I think my grandma's is better.

Don't Call Out!

There is one thing that makes
my teacher very cross indeed,
and if you ever talk to her
it's this advice you'll need:

You can jump up high
and roll about
but whatever you do,
  Don't
    Call
      Out!

You can swing round and round
like a roundabout
but whatever you do,
  Don't
    Call
      Out!

You can flap on the floor
like a slippery trout
but whatever you do,
  Don't
    Call
      Out!

You can fight each other
in a wrestling bout
but whatever you do,

Don't
       Call
             Out!

You can stick your fingers
up your snout
but whatever you do,
       Don't
            Call
               Out!

You can wiggle your ears
and gurn and pout
but whatever you do,
       Don't
            Call
               Out!

There is one rule you must not flout,
for if you do she's sure to shout.
so please don't be in any doubt:
Put your hand up!
       Don't
            Call
               Out!

Put your hand up!
       Don't
            Call
               Out!

Put your hand up!
       Don't
            Call
               Out!

Let's Hear it for Teachers

Let's hear it for teachers,
a curious crew.
There isn't a limit
to what they will do –

they mark all your work
and they do not despair
when you *still* cannot tell
between 'there', 'their' and 'they're'.

They tell you the same thing
again and again
while you sit staring blankly
and chewing your pen.

Sometimes their job
isn't terribly fun,
with scary inspectors
and scarier mums,

and screaming young children
and meddling MPs
picking holes in their work
like a lump of Swiss cheese.

But listen to me
for I swear that it's true:
the reason they teach is
they care about you.

The reason they get up
at stupid o'clock
is to give you the key
that will open the lock.

They're desperate to help you
to be at your best,
to be better people
(not just pass a test);

to do well, to think well
and walk tall with pride.
Let's hear it for teachers,
for ~~there~~ ~~their~~ they're on your side.

Bad Day

Michael is rampaging
through the classroom, overturning chairs,
lashing out at whoever gets in his way.

Today is one of his Bad Days.

They say he might be leaving this school;
when the teacher suggested it to his mum
she said it would be for the best.
The other children test him,
see how far they can push him
before he snaps and screams
"SHUT UP! SHUT UP!",
sending the class
into giggling fits.

When the class are working
Michael just sits.
Sometimes one of the other kids
tries to catch his eye,
causing Michael to fly
into a wild rage

and today is one of his Bad Days.
The bear has escaped its cage:

Michael piles into them
with windmilling fists,
sending a girl's head
crashing against a desk.
Yes today is a Bad Day.
The headmaster calls Michael's mum,
who comes to take him home.

I can see Michael and his mum
through the window now,
cuddling close together as they walk
across the car-park, towards the car.
It's the only time I've ever
seen him smiling.

The Most Embarrassing Moment Ever

was at the beach
I ran up to my mum
wrapped my arms around her legs
and cuddled her tight shouting
"Mummy! Mummy!"
but then I looked into the distance
and saw my mum
and my dad
and my sister
and they were pointing at me
and giggling
and the lady I'd been cuddling
started laughing too and said
"I think you've got the wrong lady"
and I wanted the sea
to wash over me
like a little sandcastle
like a shallow rockpool
and I decided
that I'd never
cuddle anyone again.

Homesick

My sister plays the tambourine
at half past ten at night.
My brother keeps on poking me
and looking for a fight.

My other brother hides my books
and steals all my stuff,
but *I'm* the one who gets told off –
I've really had enough.

The cat just keeps on screeching
and the dog has not been trained.
My levels of despair are just
too high to be maintained.

In fact I think I'll run away.
To somewhere else I'll roam.
I don't know where I'll wander
but I'm sick to death of home.

My Bottom's Gone Missing

My bottom's gone missing.
It left in the night.
I woke up in bed
with a terrible fright.

I reached down to greet it
and wish it good day,
but found that my bottom
had wandered astray.

I called for my dad and
I called for my mum –
"My bottom's gone missing!
My beautiful bum!"

They fetched me some cocoa
and, pouring a cup,
explained that bums vanish
when children grown up.

They said that it's normal.
There's no need to fear.
It's only young kiddies
who cherish their rear.

I told them my bottom
and I were in love.
My gorgeous, sweet bottom!
My darling! My dove!

They said to me firmly,
"Stop being a fool.
It's only a bottom.
Get ready for school."

I got myself dressed
with a tear in my eye.
I stepped out the door
and I started to cry.

I held up my pants
as I trudged down the street,
then tripped as my trousers
slid down to my feet.

The clouds gathered in
as I sunk to my knees.
Oh wonderful bottom!
Come back to me please!

Quite Interesting

I'm a shelf in a classroom.
My life is OK; not good, not bad –
a bit boring really.
Sometimes people put stuff on me,
and I quite like that, but I suppose
it's OK being empty too.
My life is quite uneventful.
In fact, the most interesting thing
that has ever happened to me
was when a poet visited, and told
the class to write a personification poem
about an object in the room.

Someone chose me.

That was quite interesting.

Ted

I live on top of the wardrobe,
in Danielle's old room.
She moved out years ago.
I remember her taking me to nursery,
to school
and to her friends' houses.
She used to sit with me at meals
and scream if anyone
tried to take me away.
She would never let me go.
Every day I wait for her to come back,
to hold me again,
just one more time.
She never does.
I feel lost, forgotten.
Children grow up,
but I never do.

Whenever I start crying
I say that I feel sick,
and no one knows I'm lying –
It always does the trick.

It's what I tell my teachers,
my friends, my mum and dad –
I tell them that I feel sick
when really I feel sad.

Colours

Green describes me.
It is fresh and bright and vibrant.
It is a colour that breathes oxygen
into the universe.
Green is replete with the dawning
of possibilities.
It's a new-born idea springing into life;
it's the feeling of wet grass
in summertime.

Red describes me.
It is angry, bitter, bubbling.
It is a colour that flashes a frown
and gnashes its teeth.
Red is fighting to escape its skin,
desperate to punch, kick and maim.
It's a wild tiger in a tiny cage;
it's a toddler screaming
on a supermarket floor.

Yellow describes me.
It is pale, sickly, withering.
It is a colour that remains
when the spirit has left.

Yellow is a patient
in a hospital bed.
It's the slow decay of blunted teeth;
it's your clothes coming out the dryer,
ruined.

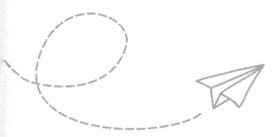

Not a Care in the World

I worry a lot.
In school we watched a programme
about the Great Plague,
and for the next few nights all I could see
were bodies, contorted and diseased
at the foot of my bed.

We talked about the Second World War,
and I worried about what I would do
if there was a war now – whether I'd be dead
and whether or not my family would survive.
I asked my mum if she was ever alive
during a war, and she said yes, of course –
there are wars going on
across the world all the time.
But what about in England? I asked.
She said she remembered the Falklands War,
which wasn't *in* England but did
involve our army.

I worry a lot.
I worry about being poor
and about famine.
On television I saw an advert asking people
to donate money to another country
where there wasn't enough to eat.
The people in the advert were covered in sheets.

63

They looked like barren winter trees.
I wondered whether my mum would be able to love me
if I looked like that, and whether
I'd be able to love her
if she did.
I've started hoarding cans of food under my bed
in case there's a famine in London.

I worry a lot.
And it isn't just big things I worry about either;
I also worry about lots and lots and lots and lots
of little things.
We had some maths homework
I didn't understand, which I worried about
until I cried over the breakfast table.
And last week I tried to write a book review
on a book I haven't even read.
I'm worried that my teacher will find out
and make me read the whole thing,
maybe even twice.
And whenever we have to get into pairs
to go on a school trip
I worry myself sick
about who I'm going to stand next to.
Sam likes girls now
so he always wants to hold a girl's hand.
James and Alex usually stand together.

So now we're on a trip and my heart
is a hammer in my chest. We're standing
in the line, two abreast –
I've been worrying about this for weeks.
The birds of anxiety peck at me with their beaks
as two old ladies pass us on the street,
eyeing us as though
they want to pinch our cheeks.
Then one turns to the other and says

"it must be great being a kid, mustn't it?
Not a care in the world."

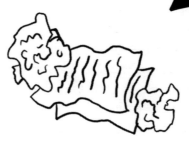

Brothers

Baby brothers
Little brothers
Handkerchief-and-spittle brothers

Bad brothers
Mean brothers
Wish-I'd-never-seen brothers

Silly brothers
Dumb brothers
Tell-on-you-to-Mum brothers

Jealous brothers
Crying brothers
Lashing out and lying brothers

Naughty brothers
Tough brothers
"Stop I've had enough" brothers

Fab brothers
Fun brothers
Going-for-a-run-brothers

Laughing brothers
Caring brothers
Generous and sharing brothers

Loving brothers
Loyal brothers
Help-you-with-your-toil brothers

Blood brothers
True brothers
None as good as you, brother.

The Day the Poet Came

The windows burped,
the hamster flew,
the walls spun round,
the grass turned blue,
things happened that
we never knew
the day the poet came.

The sky fell in,
the clouds dispersed,
the devils smiled,
the angels cursed,
the world inhaled,
began to burst
the day the poet came.

My desk became
a sailing boat,
an oak tree grew
inside my coat,
my friend got married
to a goat
the day the poet came.

The carpet turned
into a bath,
I think I saw
a pink giraffe,
but the strangest thing:
our teacher laughed
the day the poet came!

Get Writing!

Hello! Joshua here. I had a lot of fun writing the poems in this book, and I hope you have had even more fun reading them. Perhaps you saw the title of the book and thought that you really don't like poetry. If that was the case, then I hope this book has shown you that poetry can, sometimes, be a little bit enjoyable.

Now that you've discovered how fun poetry can be, why not have a go at writing some of your own? Here are some suggestions to get you started.

I Don't Like Poetry

Of course it's not true that I don't like poetry. The poem that gives this book its title is a joke: I explain why I don't like poetry in the form of a poem! In the poem, I say I don't like lots of other things, like metaphors and similes, and I go on to use them. You could try writing your own poems explaining why you don't like metaphors, similes, alliteration and onomatopoeia. You might end up with lines like:

I don't like similes. Every time I think of one my head feels like a giant cannonball.

I don't like alliteration. I think it is overwhelmingly, ostentatiously overrated.

You could even go further than I go in my poem, and include other writing devices like assonance, personification or rhyme.

Maths Poems

Poetry doesn't have to be just for literacy lessons. In fact, you can bring poetry into almost anything. 'Summing Girls Up' is a maths poem. Have a go at writing a maths poem about yourself. Have a think about what or who makes you who you are, and turn your ideas into equations. Here are some examples about me:

Me + poetry = enthusiastic

Me − family = lonely

(Me + friends) − jealousy = content

Favourite Words

I became a poet because I love words. 'Goo' is one of my favourite words, and I wrote a whole poem about it. 'Animal House' also includes lots of amazing, wonderful words:

There's a LAMENTATION of SWANS,
and a MURMURATION of STARLINGS
and a MURDER of CROWS
in my sink.

The words in capitals are collective nouns – names for groups of things. You probably know some of these already, like swarm (of bees) and flock (of sheep). All the collective nouns in 'Animal House' are real – look them up! But you can also have a go at inventing your own collective nouns. There are no right or wrong answers; you can be as playful as you like. Here are some that I made up:

A COFFEE-CUP of TEACHERS
A CREATIVITY of POETS
A SNARL of BULLIES

Weird Love Poems

Love poems do not have to be about people. I love all sorts of things, which is why I decided to write a love letter to a lychee. Why not pick something strange and write a love poem to it? It could be your favourite food, your pet hamster, your bike, your television, your bedroom, your pillow or your glasses. It could even be your school!

Alphabetical List of Poems

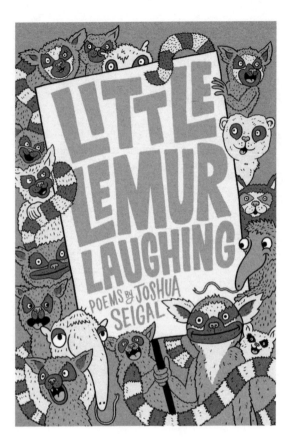

A dragon's sneeze,
a dinosaur,
a wizard's spell,
a monster's claw...
that's what's in a poem.

More fantastic poems from Joshua Seigal.

ISBN: 9781472930040

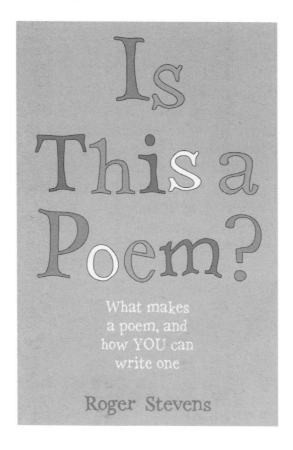

Is This a Poem?

What makes
a poem, and
how YOU can
write one

Roger Stevens

Do you like poems?
Are you sure you know what one is?!

This book is packed with every type of poem
you've ever heard of (and a few you haven't)!

ISBN: 9781472920010